YO-DWL-585

Storm Chasers

by Dan and Janet Ahearn

illustrated by Richard Kolding

TABLE OF CONTENTS

CHAPTER 1

Prairie Watch

It was a fine summer morning. As Julie Taylor ate her breakfast, she looked at her new camera. Her twin brother, Jack, sat next to her. He had a new camera, too.

The cameras were birthday presents from their parents. School had just ended for the year. It was the twins' first chance to spend the day taking pictures. The twins loved photography.

The twins often talked about how they wanted to have their pictures published in *National Geographic* magazine.

"Mom," said Jack, "Julie and I are riding our bikes out to the plains today."

"Did you check with your father? He might need help on the farm."

"We asked," said Julie. "He told us we could do whatever we wanted today."

Jack added, "He said he can't wait to see the photographs we take."

"Have you finished all of your chores?" their mom asked.

"All done, Mom."

"Already?"

"Yes, Mom," they said at the same time. They had been up before the rooster that morning.

"Well, all right," Mrs. Taylor said, "but the radio says there's a chance of thunderstorms late this afternoon. Be back here no later than 3:00. I don't want you out there if there's even a chance of lightning."

"We promise," they said.

"All right. Be sure to take your watches. Remember to check them! Don't get so caught up in your activities that you forget the time."

By the time Jack and Julie pedaled out to the plains, it was 11:00. The only clouds seemed very far away; they didn't look dangerous.

"I see a little prairie dog! There's another one! They're so cute," called Julie as she peered through a small pair of binoculars.

Jack said, "Ssshhhh! You'll scare them away!"

"See the one that's running back and forth? It looks like it's dancing," Julie giggled.

"I think it's warning the others," said Jack. "I wish they weren't so far away."

"Then let's be really quiet. We'll be able to get a closer look and take some great pictures!" Julie said.

They crept closer. As they did, the prairie dogs ducked inside their burrow. It became a game of hide-and-seek. Every time Jack and Julie tried to take a photo, the prairie dogs would run.

"Nature photography is much harder than I thought," said Jack as he laughed. Julie laughed, too.

It was as if the animals were teasing them. Every time Julie and Jack crawled closer, the little creatures ran farther away. It was frustrating but fun.

CHAPTER 2

Trouble Brewing

Suddenly, all the prairie dogs disappeared from sight. Julie looked up at the sky. It was much darker now.

"When did the clouds get so gray, Jack?" She checked her watch. "It's 3:30! We're late! Mom's going to be angry."

Jack said, "Look over there!" He pointed to some large, dark clouds that were moving very fast.

"We have to get home! We can't get caught in a thunderstorm," Julie said.

"How did this happen? How did it get so late?"

"Forget about that. Let's just get home."

The twins ran to their bicycles and headed back to the road that led to their farm. They hadn't ridden far when Jack shouted, "It looks like the storm will catch us before we reach the farm. We started too late!"

The twins pedaled as fast as they could. But they knew they couldn't beat the storm.

"It's 3:45," Julie cried.

"We're in big trouble, Julie," said Jack.

Just then they saw a lightning bolt stab
out of the clouds and touch the earth.
The twins were frightened. They both
shouted out "Wow!" at the same time.
They knew how dangerous lightning could

be. "Why didn't you keep track of the time?" asked Julie nervously.

"Why didn't *you*?" said her brother.

"Never mind," she said. "We're both to blame. Just keep going. Maybe we can beat the storm."

Jack and Julie were usually very responsible and followed instructions. They hadn't meant to ignore the time. Now they both felt they were going to pay for their mistake. They might get all wet and get sick. Their parents might ground them. They might even ruin their new cameras!

Julie and Jack kept going. Every time they looked back, the clouds seemed closer and darker.

"Jack, it might be a twister. It's so dark, and now it's getting windy."

"I know! Go faster! It's gaining on us!"

They tried. But soon their legs ached and they were out of breath. Their pedaling got slower. They were getting really tired.

Finally, Julie stopped and put her foot on the ground. Jack stopped next to her.

"We have to take cover soon, Jack. How about under that bridge? We can stay under there if we have to."

They started toward the bridge. They were tired and getting scared. It looked as if the storm were about to catch them.

Finally, they reached the bridge and walked their bikes underneath.

"Look, Jack. What are those people doing?"

They could see a van parked by the side of the road. There were five people standing beside it.

"Maybe they can help us," said Jack. "They don't seem worried about the storm at all."

Although the storm was bearing down on them, the group had set up lots of strange equipment. There were two large radar dishes on a tripod. The twins thought each dish looked like the satellite TV dish on the roof of their house.

Happy to see some other people, the twins walked their bikes over to them. Everyone was so busy that no one noticed them.

The twins saw a young woman taping the storm with a video camera. It was their neighbor Cassie Jones, who was home from college and working for the summer.

They both called out, "Cassie!"

She turned and saw the twins. "Jack? Julie?" Cassie said in disbelief. "What are you doing out here! It's very dangerous! You can't outrun a tornado on a bike!"

The twins looked at each other. "Tornado!" they said.

That's when the reality of the situation hit them. They were in danger.

CHAPTER 3

Twister!

Cassie was worried about the twins' safety. But her team couldn't stop yet. She told the twins to get in the van. She ordered the twins to stay out of the way and let the team work.

Julie and Jack watched them but didn't really understand what they were doing. Then Julie realized that they were measuring the storm.

An older woman seemed to be in charge. She was shouting orders and advice over the growing noise of the storm. The twins could almost feel the storm pressing down on them. Dust started to fly around outside.

They saw Cassie and the others put on safety goggles to protect their eyes from the dust. They also saw that a lot of dust

17

was being drawn up into the air beneath the storm.

Suddenly, one of the team shouted, "Here we go!"

"Twister! Hot dog!" shouted Cassie. The twins had to admit that they felt safer inside the van.

But they also wanted to get closer to the windows to get a better look. Both agreed not to. They decided that they were in too much trouble already.

Suddenly, in the distance, a whirling spiral of dust and water rose into the air. It slowly formed the funnel of the tornado. Julie thought the tornado looked like a giant's finger slowly poking down from the swirling clouds in the distance.

The finger grew thicker and longer until it touched the ground. It cast up great dust clouds as it stirred up the dirt.

Outside, everyone was shouting with excitement.

Julie and Jack couldn't stand it. They had to get a better view of the tornado. They opened the door of the van just enough so that they could take some pictures. They just kept snapping away at the incredible sight.

Cassie turned and saw that the twins were leaning out of the door.

"I told you two to stay in the van! I know it's exciting, but I don't want you getting hurt! In the van, now!" She angrily slammed the door.

Suddenly, the man operating the instrument with the two radar dishes shouted, "I think we should go while the going is good!" The tornado showed no sign of breaking up. The twister was coming!

The men picked up the twins' bikes and tied them on top of the van. Cassie jumped inside with the others and they sped away from the storm.

They drove down the road and stopped under the same bridge that the twins had found. Luckily, though, they didn't need shelter. The tornado broke up. There was a brief downpour of rain, but finally, the sun came out.

Cassie turned to the twins and said, "Your parents are probably worried sick about you. What were you doing out in a storm like that?"

The twins looked away, embarrassed. "We lost track of the time," Julie said.

Cassie asked what they were doing on the prairie. They explained and told Cassie how difficult it was to photograph prairie dogs.

"What were *you* doing out there, Cassie?" said Julie.

"Scientific research," she said. "We chase these storms. We try to catch a tornado forming, just the way we did today. Then we measure it. The more we know about these storms, the better we can protect people from them." Then she added, "I can't believe you two took pictures through the whole thing."

"We want to be professionals," said Julie.

"We tried to stay calm," Jack said. "I guess it takes practice."

Both admitted they were happy to be going home.

As they neared the farm, the twins saw their mother coming down the road in the station wagon. When they jumped out of the van, Mrs. Taylor threw her arms around both of them.

Cassie offered to develop the twins' tornado photos with the team's pictures. The twins happily agreed.

The next morning, Cassie stopped by with a copy of the local newspaper.

Cassie said, "Can you believe it? Our film was damaged. Your tornado pictures were so good that I took them over to the newspaper. Look, now you really are professionals!"

There, on the front page, were two large photographs of the tornado. Under each photo it read, "Photographs by Julie Taylor and Jack Taylor." The twins were really excited.

Then they saw the headline. It read, "CLOSE CALL!" They looked at each other and said, "And how!"